Nellie Lou's Hairdos

John Sandford

Little, Brown and Company
Boston Toronto London

To
Mary,
with admiration
and
a permanent
wave.
—j.s.

ISBN: 0-316-77080-9
Library of Congress Catalog Card Number 88-40619

10 9 8 7 6 5 4 3 2
MAN
Published simultaneously in Canada by
Little, Brown & Company (Canada) Limited

Printed in Hong Kong

Mrs. Kerchoo's Hair Shop is the best hair shop in town.
It is also the *only* hair shop in town.

Every day after school, Mrs. Kerchoo's daughter Nellie Lou
stops by the shop to help.

One day, Mrs. Kerchoo said to her daughter, "Nellie Lou, I have some errands to do. Since it's not busy now, will you do me a favor and watch the shop?"

Nellie Lou smiled and said, "Sure!"

As soon as Mrs. Kerchoo left the shop, Miss Gump walked in.
"I *must* have a new hairdo, and I must have it *right now!*"

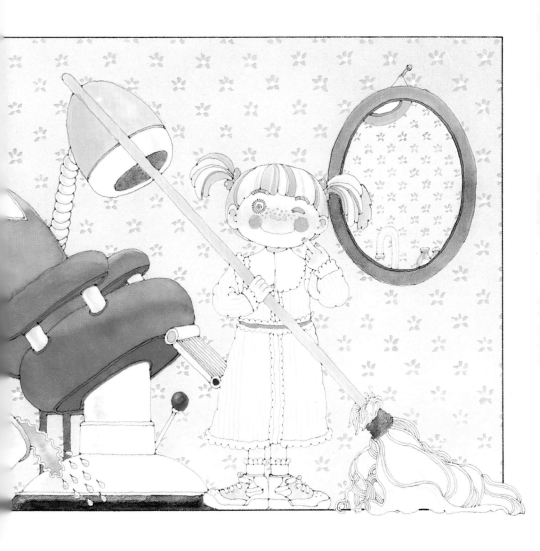

Nellie Lou thought, "I will help Miss Gump, and I will
help my mom, too." But Nellie Lou didn't know that
Miss Gump could never, *ever* make up her mind.

Miss Gump sat down in the chair and picked up a newspaper. "Go to it, Nellie Lou," she said.

Nellie Lou picked up a brush. She flipped, frizzed, and fluffed Miss Gump's hair into a lovely style.

"It is truly very nice, Nellie Lou, but can you do something...sweeter?" asked Miss Gump.

Nellie Lou went back to work. She teased, twisted, and knotted Miss Gump's hair. "A beehive! This is a *honey* of a hairdo. But can you make it more...island breezy?" asked Miss Gump.

Nellie Lou made it more island breezy.
But Miss Gump frowned.
"How about something…Swiss cheesy?"
asked Miss Gump.

"This isn't right," Miss Gump sadly said.
"Maybe a style to keep the heat off my head?"

But for Miss Gump, this style was not better.
So Nellie Lou tried a style that was wetter.

Miss Gump sighed.
"Maybe I need something that looks kind of royal...."

So Nellie Lou made little jewels of foil.

Then Miss Gump said, "I hate to be a pain,
but will this stand up in the pouring rain?"

So Nellie Lou piled Miss Gump's hair up high
so that it would keep her protected and dry.

Miss Gump turned her head and she let out a sigh.
Her hair was then styled for the Fourth of July.

Miss Gump squinched her nose.
She gasped and then frowned.
So Nellie Lou crafted a merry-go-round.

Nellie Lou worked on and on, hairdo after hairdo.
But for Miss Gump, each hairdo would *not* do.

She made fast hairdos and slow hairdos,

old hairdos and new hairdos.

She tried shoe-dos, moo-dos, and food-dos,

chair-dos, bear-dos, and pear-dos.

Nellie Lou thought, "I *like* to do hairdos.
But these are 'dos I *don't* like to do."

Miss Gump moaned. "Oh, Nellie Lou,
what *else* can you do?
I *must* have something *new!*"
Then Nellie Lou knew *just* what to do.

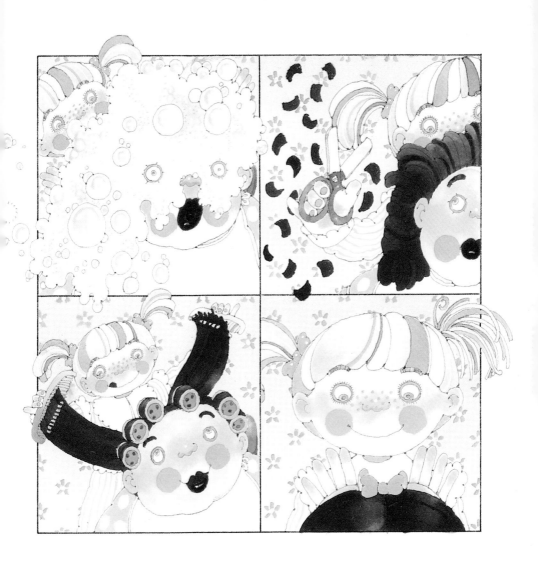

Nellie Lou washed, colored, and dried Miss Gump's hair.
Then she cut, curled, and combed it. She put a pink
bow on top. Finally, Miss Gump's hair was perfect.

"It is truly wonderful," said Miss Gump as she left the shop.
"Thank you, Nellie Lou."

Nellie Lou was very happy to see Miss Gump
pleased with her "new" hairdo. But she was even
happier to see Miss Gump *leave*.

Nellie Lou did her best to clean up the shop.

Just as she was putting away the last curler,
Mrs. Kerchoo walked in.

"Did anything happen while I was out, Nellie Lou?"
her mother asked.
"Oh…" said Nellie Lou, "nothing much.…"